Rocks! Rocks! Rocks!

Written and Illustrated by

Nancy Elizabeth Wallace

Marshall Cavendish Children

Marshall Cavendish Corporation, 99 White Plains Road, Tarrytown, NY 10591
www.marshallcavendish.us/kids

Library of Congress Cataloging-in-Publication Data
Wallace, Nancy Elizabeth.
Rocks! rocks! rocks! / by Nancy Elizabeth Wallace.
p. cm.
ISBN 978-0-7614-5528-8
1. Rocks—Juvenile literature. I. Title.
QE432.2.W347 2008
552—dc22
2008006482

The art is rendered in origami and other papers, and photographs.
Book design by Virginia Pope
Editor: Margery Cuyler

Printed in China
First edition
3 5 6 4 2

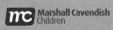

FOR:

Amy, Bebe, Bobbi, Carol, Claudia, Cyd,
Debbie, Donna, Jan, Janet, Robin, Sally, Sarah;

Doe, Leslie B., Leslie C., Judy, Kay, Lorraine,
Mary-Kelly, Nancy A.;

Bina, Kate D., Kate F., Lynn;

Margery, Anahid, Brian, Virginia,
Richard, Sean, Alan, Marilyn,
and George;

and *always* for Peter
and my Mom, Alexine—
YOU ROCK!
love,
N.E.W.

One day after school Buddy took six rocks out of his backpack. He carefully piled one on top of another. They wobbled but didn't fall. "Look!" he said to Mama.

Buddy's Trail Mix
chocolate chips, dried cranberries, dried pineapple, raisins, dried banana chips, sunflower seeds

"That looks like a pile of rocks that marks a trail," said Mama. "Would you like to go on a rock walk at the Nature Center?"

"Yes!" said Buddy. "I like rocks!"

They drove to the Nature Center. The sky was filled with billowy clouds. The air smelled of pine trees.

"Rocks!" shouted Buddy.

 "The Blue Diamond Trail," said Mama.

Welcome to
**Rock Ridge
Nature Center.**
Enjoy your visit.
The Rock Ridge Rangers

Trails

⬤ **Yellow Circle**
   Forest Trail   ⬅

⬛ **Red Square**
   Pond Trail   ⬇

◆ **Blue Diamond**
   Rock Trail   ➡

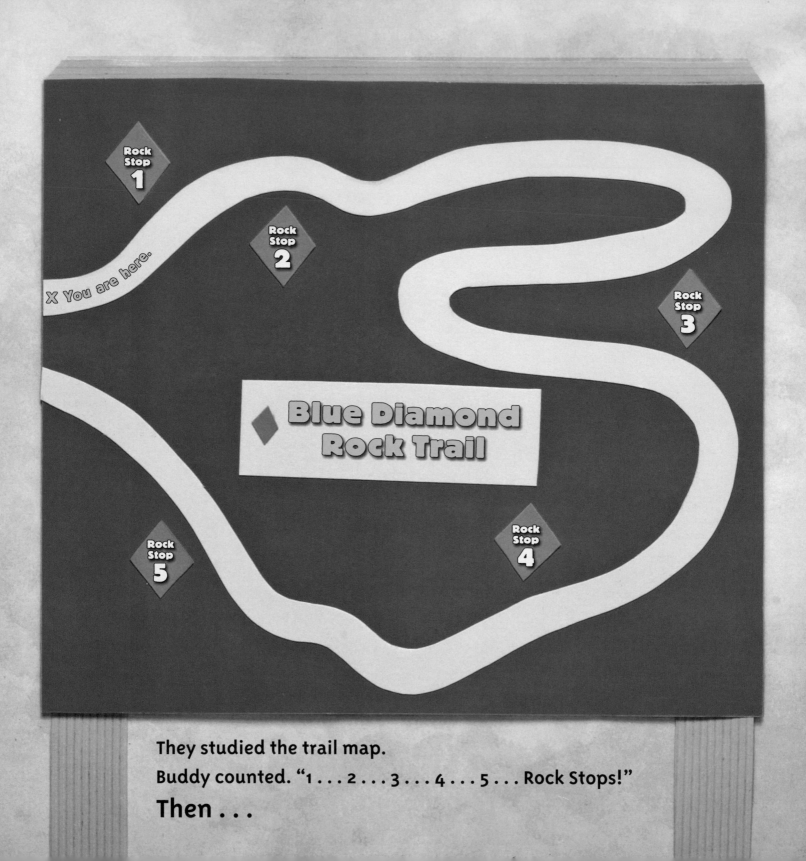

They studied the trail map.

Buddy counted. "1 . . . 2 . . . 3 . . . 4 . . . 5 . . . Rock Stops!"

Then . . .

. . . they followed the Blue Diamond Trail.

"Look!" said Buddy. "There's a pile of rocks like the one I made! This way!"

Did you know?
There are more than
100 kinds of rocks.

"Rock Stop One," said Mama. "Bedrock."

Buddy ran his hand over the smooth rock. "Bedrock! What's bedrock?"

"Bedrock is the earth's rock crust," said Mama. "Mountains are rock. Rock is under cities and farms, under valleys and forests, under lakes—"

"Under the ocean and under our house?" asked Buddy.

"Yes," said Mama. "Bedrock is everywhere. The earth is a ball of rock."

Rock
Stop
1
Bedrock

The **earth** is a ball of **rock**.

"Mama?"
"Yes, Bud."
"What did the pebble sleep on?"
"What?"
"BEDrock!"
Mama laughed.
Then . . .

Rock Stop 2 Erosion

. . . they followed the Blue Diamond Trail.

"Rock Stop Two," said Buddy.
"Big rocks, smaller rocks, and pebbles!"
"Erosion," said Mama.
"E - ROW - shun," said Buddy.
"What's that?"

Mama explained. "Erosion means that over time, mountains . . . boulders . . . even pebbles weather and wear away. They get smaller and—"

Buddy chimed in. "Smaller and smaller." He thought for a minute. "How small?"

"As small as sand and dirt. Sand and dirt are partly made of teeny, tiny pieces of rock!"

Did you know? There are many kinds of sand and dirt because there are different kinds of rocks in different places.

Mama read the sign. "What causes erosion?"

Buddy looked at the pictures. "Rain . . . snow?"

"That's right!" said Mama. "Snow and ice can get into cracks in rocks and split them."

"Rivers . . . waterfalls . . . waves," said Buddy. "Hey, I think those are all *water*!"

"I think you are very smart," said Mama. "Moving water wears down rocks."

Can you guess?

Buddy kept looking. "Wind?"

Mama explained. "Wind causes waves that make rocks tumble on the shores of lakes and oceans. Tumbling wears down rocks. Strong winds can also blow sand at rocks and wear them away."

"Sun?" asked Buddy.

"The sun heats rocks during the day. The rocks cool off at night. Heating and cooling makes rocks break apart," said Mama.

"Roots?"

"Plants and tree roots can split rocks, too!" said Mama.

"WOW!" said Buddy. "I thought rocks lasted forever!"

Then . . .

. . . they followed the Blue Diamond Trail.

To Rock Stop 3

Rock
Stop
3
How Rocks
Are Formed

At Rock Stop 3 they were greeted by one of the Rock Ridge Rangers.

"Hello! Welcome to Rock Stop Three. I'm Roxie," she said.

"Hi! I'm Buddy."

"Well, Buddy," said Roxie. "I've got some wonderful rocks to show you."

Roxie took three rocks out of her rock box. She handed one to Buddy.

"I see layers," said Buddy.

"That's a sedimentary rock," said Roxie. "It's made from sediment."

"SED - uh - ment," said Buddy. "What's that?"

"Sediment is teeny, tiny particles of rock, clay, mud, and sand. Sedimentary rocks are made from layers and layers of sediment that were pressed and hardened," said Roxie. "Over time the sediment became hard . . . as . . . a . . ."

"Rock!" said Buddy.

"Here's another sedimentary rock," said Roxie.

"It's crumbly!" said Buddy.

"Some rocks are softer than others," said Roxie. "This rock is *sand*stone."

"Roxie?"

"Yes, Buddy."

"What did Sandy the stone like to sit in?"

"What?"

"A ROCKing chair!"

"Good one, Buddy," said Roxie.

"I bet you know what this is."

"Chalk," said Buddy.

"Chalk is sedimentary rock, too," said Roxie. "It's lime*stone*."

Roxie reached into the rock box again.

"A blackboard!" said Buddy.

"It's slate," said Roxie. "Slate is one kind of metamorphic rock."

"Met - a - MORE - fick!" said Buddy.

"Metamorphic rocks are rocks that changed. This was once mudstone—stone made from mud. Over time it changed into slate."

Buddy thought for a minute. "Rocks can change?"

"Yes!" said Roxie. "Deep inside the earth, heat and *squeeeeezing* can change rocks."

Roxie

Rock Ridge Ranger's
Rock Box

Roxie took more rocks
out of the rock box.

"These are igneous rocks."

"Can we call them Iggy for short?" asked Buddy.

Roxie handed one to Buddy. "Sure. Iggy rocks are formed in the heat way, way, way deep down inside the earth. It is so hot that rocks melt!"

"Rocks can melt?" asked Buddy

"Yes!" said Roxie. "And flow like a hot, rock river. Can you see where melted rock flowed and filled in cracks, then cooled?"

"Yes!" said Buddy.

Next Roxie pulled a plastic container and a canteen out of the rock box. Buddy poured water into the container.

"Put this rock in the water," said Roxie.

Rock Ridge Ranger's
Rock Box

Roxie

"It floats! How can a rock float?" asked Buddy.

Roxie explained. "This igneous rock came from a volcano. It's filled with bubbles. It's light enough to float."

"Wow!" said Buddy.

Roxie gave Buddy a sticker. He stuck it to his shirt. "I'm a Rock Star!"

They put the rocks back into the rock box. Buddy and Mama said good-bye to Roxie.

Then . . .

. . . they followed the Blue Diamond Trail until they came to Rock Stop 4.

There were lots of rocks set out on a red table.

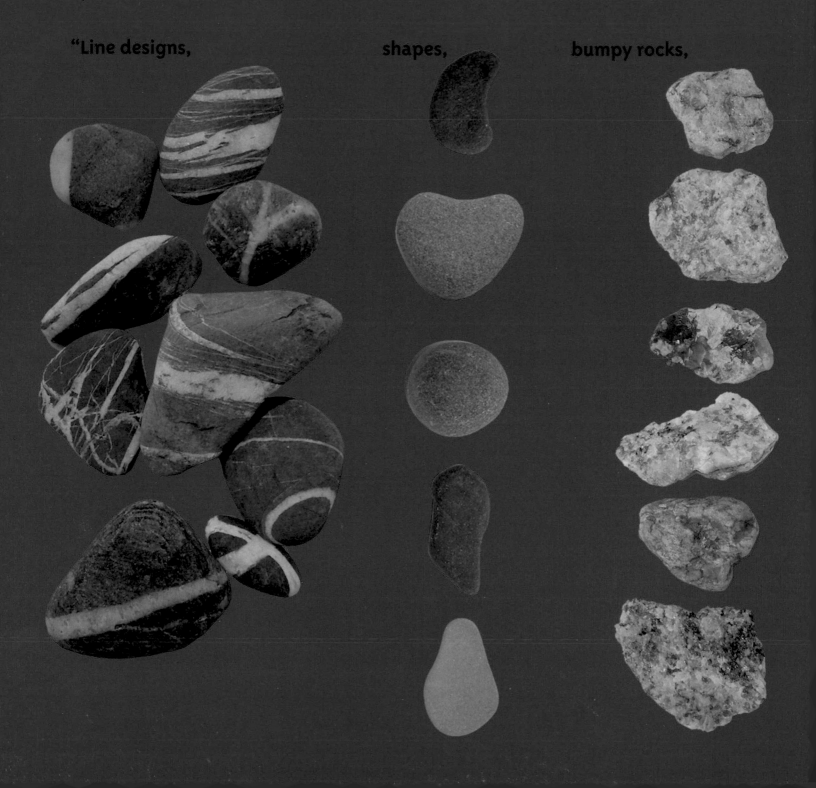

Buddy sorted them.

"Line designs,   shapes,   bumpy rocks,

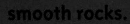
smooth rocks.

The smooth rocks look like eggs!" said Buddy.

"They were tumbled by ocean waves and smoothed by sand and pebbles rubbing against them," said Mama.

Buddy counted the smooth ones.

. . . then another.

"Mama, what kind of candy did the pebble like to eat for dessert?"
"What?"
"ROCK candy!"
Mama chuckled. She looked at her watch. "Dessert! We better get moving. It's almost time for dinner!"

Buddy put the rocks back in a pile.
Then . . .

. . . they followed the Blue Diamond Trail.

"A little house!" said Buddy.

Rock
Stop
5
Building with
Rocks

"Where do you see rocks?" asked Mama.

"The chimney! The stone wall! Where do *you* see rocks?" asked Buddy.

"I see a slate rock roof and bricks made out of clay," said Mama. "And I'm sitting on a rock bench."

"I see a birdbath made out of rock," said Buddy. "And a rock frog!"

"I see it's time to go home, my young petrologist," said Mama.

Take a rock walk
where you live.

What rocks
do you see?

"What's a pet - trol - o - gist ?" asked Buddy.
"Someone who has a pet?"
 "Someone like you, who likes to learn about rocks,"
said Mama.

RECYCLE

Trash Please

They read the last two signs.

Then Buddy said, "Mama?"

"Yes, Bud."

"How did the boulder get to the moon?"

"How?"

"On a ROCKet!"

Did you know?
A meterorite is a rock from outer space.

Thank you
for visiting today!

*The Rock Ridge
Rangers*

ROCK
STAR

Start a rock collection

Collect small rocks that you like.
Wash the rocks in water and let them dry.

Display the rocks on a shelf or in a clear plastic jar
or glue your rock collection to the inside top of a sturdy cardboard box.

Make Rock Magnets

You will need:

    magnet tape from a craft store

    scissors

    non-toxic glue

    small, flat rocks

1. Wash and dry the rocks.
2. Ask an adult to help with the next step. Cut pieces of magnet tape that fit the backs of your rocks.
3. Glue a magnet to the back of each rock.

Rock magnets make great gifts!

ROCK Sayings

You rock! *You're cool.*

Rock on. *Keep going.*

It's just a stone's throw from here. *It's very close by.*

You've got rocks in your head. *You think another person's idea doesn't make sense.*

You're a chip off the old rock. *You're just like your mom and dad.*

Rocky Names in Rocky Places

Boulder, Colorado

Flint, Michigan

Goose Rock, Kentucky

Granite Falls, Washington

Little Rock, Arkansas

Pebble Beach, California

Pipestone, Manitoba

Rock Bluff, Florida

Rockford, Illinois

Rockland, Ontario

Rocky Bottom, South Carolina

Rocky Point, British Columbia

Shiprock, New Mexico

Stoneman Lake, Arizona

Stony Hollow, New York

Stony River, Alaska

Yellowstone National Park

Do you know others?

Make up a rock joke.

Build a rock trail marker.

Find several rocks.

Try to stack up six of them!

A rock trail marker is also called a cairn (karn).